To Jett,

my HP buddy,

and to my children,

who make life

MAGICAL.

GROSSET & DUNLAP
Penguin Young Readers Group
An Imprint of Penguin Random House LLC

Text and illustrations copyright © 2017 by Ashley Evanson. All rights reserved. Published by Grosset & Dunlap, an imprint of Penguin Random House LLC,
345 Hudson Street, New York, New York 10014. GROSSET & DUNLAP is a trademark of Penguin Random House LLC. Manufactured in China.

Library of Congress Cataloging-in-Publication Data is available.

ISBN 9780399543920   10 9 8 7 6 5 4 3 2 1

THIS BOOK IS MAGIC

by Ashley Evanson

Grosset & Dunlap
An Imprint of Penguin Random House

Do you know you have a magic finger?
Yes, you! Give it a wave.

See this hat?
Tap it three times with your magic finger
and say the magic word:

Let's try it again.
These books are too small. Give your finger a swish
in the air and say:

BIBBIDI BOBBIDI... BIG!

Underwater Sea Creatures

POTIONS

Magic Spells

PLANTS

You're getting pretty good.
Let's try something harder.

Wave your finger high above
your head and say:

Nicely done!

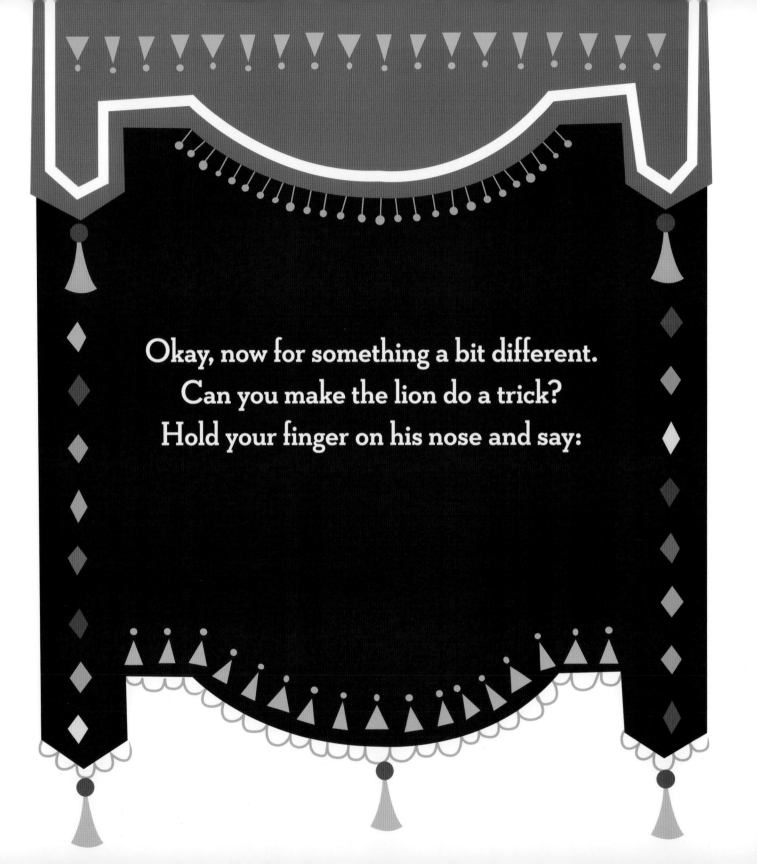

Okay, now for something a bit different.
Can you make the lion do a trick?
Hold your finger on his nose and say:

HOCUS POCUS!

TA-DA!

You let the lion out of his cage.
Look at him juggle!

Let's move on to something trickier.
This frog used to be a prince.
Let's turn him back to his old self.
Rub the pink potion bottle and say:

SHAZAM!

Oops, wrong potion.

Rub this blue bottle and say it again.

SHAZAM!

Excellent!

It's the queen of hearts.
Why don't we give this card a new look?
Twirl your finger over the card and say:

PRESTO CHANGE-O!

Now it's the cupcake of hearts!

Tasty! Let's make more.

Wiggle your magic finger and say:

A LA DESSERT!

Ooh la la!
Lots of desserts!

And now, for the grand finale,
tap each firework with your finger and say:

FINITO!

Amazing! Bet you were wondering where the ship went.

You really are good at magic!